JUNIPER HOLLOW

Fox and Raccoon

Lesley-Anne Green

tundra

Tundra Books, an imprint of Penguin Random House Canada Young Readers, a
Penguin Random House Company

Library and Archives Canada Cataloguing in Publication

Green, Lesley-Anne, 1977–, author, illustrator
     Fox and raccoon / Lesley-Anne Green.

Issued in print and electronic formats.
ISBN 978-1-101-91796-1 (hardcover).—ISBN 978-1-101-91798-5 (EPUB)

     I. Title.

PS8613.R42823F69 2018   jC813'.6   C2017-903019-1
                                                 C2017-903020-5

Published simultaneously in the United States of America by Tundra Books of
Northern New York, an imprint of Penguin Random House Canada Young Readers,
a Penguin Random House Company

Library of Congress Control Number: 2017940552

Edited by Samantha Swenson
Designed by Rachel Cooper
Juniper branches © AllNikArt/Shutterstock.com
The artwork in this book was rendered in needle-felted wool, balsa wood and fabric.
The text was set in Plantin MT Pro.

Printed and bound in China

www.penguinrandomhouse.ca

1   2   3   4   5   22   21   20   19   18

Penguin
Random House
TUNDRA BOOKS

For Gus and Jeff

Fox and Raccoon lived in a quiet little corner of Juniper Hollow.

They had been best friends and neighbors for as long as they could remember.

Now don't get me wrong—they had their ups and downs and their down and outs, but they always managed to work it out. That's just what best friends do!

Fox and Raccoon played together every day: hopscotch, chase, hide-and-seek. And sometimes they liked to just lie in the grass and relax.

On this particular occasion, Raccoon thought the day would unfold like any other, but something else was in store for our furry friend . . .

When Raccoon arrived at Fox's house as usual that morning, Fox did not look like she was ready for a day of fun and games.

"I'm sorry, Raccoon. I'm just too busy to come out and play today," said Fox.

Well, Raccoon knew that four paws are better than two when it comes to doing chores, so he grabbed a stack of letters from the table and zoomed off!

Raccoon took those letters all the way to the post office.

"My, my, you sure do have a lot of friends, Raccoon," said Postmaster Beaver, looking at the large stack of letters.

"Oh, these aren't mine," explained Raccoon proudly, "I'm mailing them for Fox!"

Raccoon was so happy to have helped out that he skipped all the way back to Fox's house. Maybe now she would have time to play!

But when Raccoon got back to Fox's house, Fox was even more tied up than before.

"I mailed your letters for you," said Raccoon. "Is there anything else I can help you with? You seem awful busy."

"That's kind of you to offer, but I'm almost done. I just have to go buy a couple more eggs so that I can fin—"

But before Fox could finish her sentence, Raccoon was already out the door.

"You stay here! I'll be right back!" he yelled over his shoulder.

Raccoon scampered on over to Hedgehog's farm stand.

"One basket of eggs, please," said Raccoon.

"Whatcha cookin' up today?" asked Hedgehog.

"Oh, I'm not cooking anything, but Fox is! These are for her," said Raccoon. He didn't know what Fox was making, but he was sure that whatever it was, it would be delicious!

Raccoon walked very carefully all the way back to Fox's; he wanted to make sure those eggs were safe and sound so that Fox could finish her baking.

When Raccoon returned, though, Fox was already working on something else.

"Here are your eggs, Fox," he said. "What's that you're making?"

"Oh thank you, Raccoon! You're always saving the day," she said. "I'm making juniper juice, but I seem to have run out of berries."

"Berries?" Raccoon said. "Coming right up!"

Raccoon knew just the place to pick the best berries in town — Badger's Berry Patch!

When Raccoon arrived at the berry patch, it was a hustle and bustle of critters, baskets and berries.

"What kind of berries you lookin' for today?" boomed Badger. "We've got blueberries, blackberries, gooseberries, huckleberries—"

"Excuse me," Raccoon interrupted politely. "Do you happen to have any juniper berries?"

"Why, of course we do," Badger said. "Right this way!"

Raccoon got down to work and picked two baskets of berries in no time!

He hurried back to Fox's house as quickly as he could, trying not to eat too many berries along the way!

Raccoon arrived back at the house to find Fox in the middle of yet another project.

"My goodness, you sure do have your paws full today," said Raccoon. And without needing to be asked, he jumped right in. Crafting is one of his specialties, and he was happy to help!

"Oh dear!" said Fox, noticing that Raccoon had got himself into a bit of a bind. She thought for a moment. "Looks like I'm going to need some more yarn," she said. "But Cat lives all the way across town."

"Don't worry!" said Raccoon. "I'll go!"

Fox shook her head and smiled as her friend raced away.

Cat is the best knitter in Juniper Hollow and always happy to share her yarn. When Raccoon explained the situation, she told him that he could take as much as he liked. That's how things are in Juniper Hollow — friends like to help friends out. Raccoon chose a beautiful green yarn because that's Fox's favorite color.

Raccoon had almost arrived back at Fox's when he noticed some flowers growing nearby. He thought maybe he'd bring Fox some flowers to surprise her. And do you know what that Raccoon did? He set to work picking the sweetest, prettiest flowers he could find and completely forgot about the time!

When he arrived back at Fox's, it was getting late. The house looked dark and empty. Raccoon was a little worried . . . where could Fox be?

Raccoon was thrilled. A surprise party, for him?! He'd had
so much fun helping Fox, he'd forgotten it was his birthday.
But that's just the kind of friend he is.

"I can't believe you did all of this for me!" said Raccoon.

"I didn't do it alone," she said. "We did it together . . . just like we always do!"